Peedie

Olivier Dunrea

WALKER BOOKS
AND SUBSIDIARIES
LONDON · BOSTON · SYDNEY · AUCKLAND

First published in Great Britain 2005 by Walker Books Ltd
87 Vauxhall Walk, London SE11 5HJ

This edition published 2006

2 4 6 8 10 9 7 5 3 1

© 2004 Olivier Dunrea
Published by arrangement with Houghton Mifflin Company

This book has been typeset in Shannon

Printed in China

British Library Cataloguing in Publication Data:
a catalogue record for this book is available from the British Library

ISBN-13: 978-1-4063-0138-0
ISBN-10: 1-4063-0138-8

www.walkerbooks.co.uk

For Lily and Bobby

This is Peedie.

Peedie is a gosling.

A small, yellow gosling
who sometimes forgets things.

Peedie forgets things.
Even when Mama Goose reminds him.

He forgets to come in
out of the rain.

He forgets to eat all his food.

He forgets to tidy his nest.

He forgets to take a nap.

He forgets to turn the egg.

But Peedie never forgets to wear
his lucky red baseball cap.

He wears it everywhere he goes.

He wears it when he dives.

He wears it when he slides.

He wears it when he explores.

He wears it when he snores.

Peedie never forgets to wear his
lucky red baseball cap.

Everywhere he goes.

Then one day Peedie put his lucky
red baseball cap in a secret place.

But he forgot where he put it.

He looked in the pond.

He looked in the apples.

He looked under the flower pot.

He looked in the tall grass.

But Peedie could not remember
where he had put it.

"Did you forget to turn the egg?"
Mama Goose asked.

Peedie slowly trudged to the nest.
His lucky red baseball cap was gone.

Then he saw it.
"There you are!" he said.

Peedie is a gosling.
A small, yellow gosling
who forgets things – sometimes!